IN PURSUIT

of

YOU

The Awakening

STEPHANIE L. WILLIAMS

GWW
PUBLISHING CO.

GWW Publishing
PO Box 291764
Columbia, SC 29229

ISBN-13: 978-0-9991975-4-7

DEDICATION

I dedicate to YOU. The person YOU truly are. Pursue YOU, never let a day go by that you are not discovering your authentic self. YOU are worth it.

PREFACE

After waking up at forty-three years of age God revealed to me that I was dancing with my purpose, but I never fully embraced it. Now to some, the question may be asked "what does that mean", but to others you fully understand. Now to those who don't understand, let me explain.

Being a minister, I knew how to step in and out of my purpose yet hold the silhouette before me that I was always in it. I would do the things that would tap my purpose on the should to hit to it that I wanted to dance, but when purpose fully turned around I would dance with it not fully touching it, not fully embracing its strength, nor allowing its need of me to emerge within.

Many would say, "Didn't your pursuit begin from birth?" Yes, it did. Before I was formed in the womb of my mother, God had already predestined who I would become. Along the way I began to come into the knowledge of who I was to become, but it wasn't until I turned forty-three that I awaken into the fullness of who I am.

Walking through this pursuit of myself may upset some, offend a few or even disturbed the nosey. But no one's journey is perfect and every battle won brought me that much closer to my expected end…

Society tells you that at 18 you are an adult. You are able to legally sign contracts without the consent of your parents. You are able to do things that others can legally do, except drink. Most often than not, you take this new found freedom to explore life, never really taking into consideration of who you truly are. You will step into this new freedom, embracing it fully. Happy to no longer require the approval of your parents, but to taste every delectable aspect of what society calls life.

Then it happens. Life. Situations, problems and or issues come into your life that momma and daddy didn't prepare you for. You find yourself going down a road that leads you totally away from the dreams of the little girl or boy you once had. What or who got you off course? Why did your dreams die?

DADDY ISSUES

My daddy issues didn't occur because I didn't have a father in the home, just the opposite. My father and mother were married, in the same home raising me and my sisters. Being the oldest, I always felt weird. Like, I felt like I didn't fit in my family. I wanted to do things alone, not really be a part of my family. I never understood why.

My father was closer, I felt, to my sisters. They were daddy's girls. I couldn't seem to get that close to my father. Not that I didn't want to be, but I wouldn't allow myself to open up. I closed off because I was the independent one and felt I could do it all myself.

When it came time for me to start dating, I never had the conversation with my dad about boys. So I didn't know how I was supposed to be treated. I didn't know I was supposed to be cherished and not tarnished. I didn't know that the very essence of me I was supposed to save and not expose it, trying to see if it would bring me love.

When I because a "woman" or so I thought, I allowed the words of men to entice my heart into believing their kind of love was real. I gave them what I thought would keep them close and would cause them to love me back. Funny thing was, every time I gave my essence away, I wasn't refilled, but left empty. Yet every time I heard the words "I love you" I would allow the male in my life at that time to release himself in me. I being naïve thought it was two people having sex, but actually what took place was this and every man after him releasing his entire being into me.

The only way I knew that a man "loved" me was to have sex with him. By having sex, to me it meant commitment, togetherness, and oneness. The reality of it was I was the only one committed, they on the

4

other hand were not. I began to believe that sex was the key to establishing the foundation of a relationship. Trust me it wasn't. What it became was a downward spiral of my self-esteem, confidence, and my relationship with God.

I needed the validation of a man to make me feel like I was truly a woman. I would submerge my total being into making the "sexship" work. Even if that meant diminishing who I was as a woman so that he could feel or think that he was truly a man.

** **Sexship**- *The act of engaging into sexual activities with the opposite and/or same sex, purely for fleshly gratification.*

I was looking for love through sex, seeking approval of who I was then through connection, never once taking the time to go to my dad and ask him, why this or that. I had shut myself off from developing a true father daughter relationship with him. My dad didn't have issues being my father, but I had issues being a daughter. My daddy issues over took who I was becoming.

Now I know you are wondering what did I do to get over my daddy issues. I began to learn who I was.

I was so broken that I didn't know that over the years the love I was seeking was always with me. My father loved me but I thought that love should look like a scene from the Cosby Show. I was living a reality life, but not living in reality.

If you are using sex, manipulation, intimidation, finances to acquire love, you must take a deeper look into why.

Take the time to dig deeper into yourself to see where this type of behavior began. I begin looking for love and validation through sex was the bi-product spirit of me desiring a deeper, closer relationship with my father. Every man I laid with I assumed they could fulfill that missing piece within me, but in reality it was the creation of a person I truly didn't know but had to heal.

Every bi-product spirit has a parent spirit ~ Bishop Clinton Smith

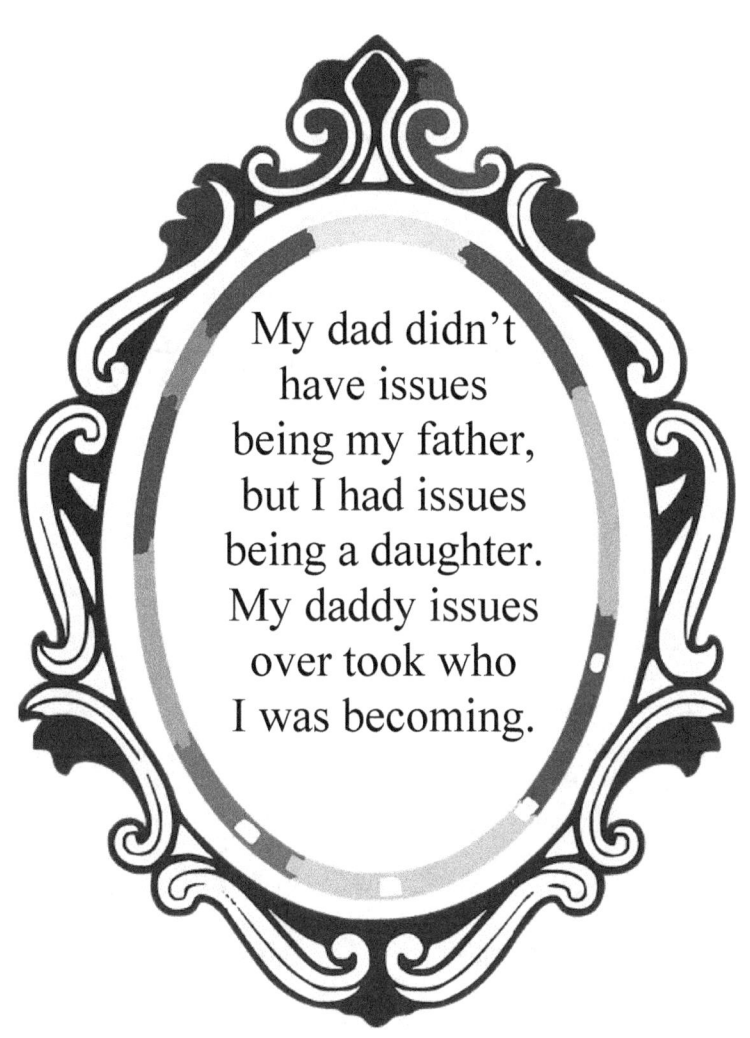

My dad didn't
have issues
being my father,
but I had issues
being a daughter.
My daddy issues
over took who
I was becoming.

CONTROL FREAK

As time progressed, I allowed my daddy issues to turn me into a control freak. I was so desperate for love that I had to be in control of how I received love and every aspect concerning of my life. I wanted the relationship to go my way and for any man that I was involved with to dance by the beat of my drum. I had begun to dummy myself down to become the type of woman that the man wanted, that I was with at the time, yet not fully giving myself to him. I would give myself sexually, but never mentally or emotionally, so I thought.

My control spewed over into my work ethic. Now someone would say, "oh, but that is a good thing." And in some cases, it could or can't be. But for me, it wasn't. It caused me to not train others in areas of my expertise. I thought training them would eliminate me. I would show only what I need to just to make it appear I had done what I needed to do to appease my employer at the time.

I had to be in control of everything I was doing. I had to control how I allowed a man to be in my life. It became such an issue, that when I wanted to end a sexship, I would initiate the final sexual encounter, be the one in control and when I was satisfied I was done. This meant I was done with the sexship, the man and anything tied to him.

I became this way because I didn't want to get hurt anymore. I had been in relationships and it ended with me being heartbroken. I could never figure out why, so I became a wall to relationships and continued to feed my flesh with what it desired.

My personal friendships suffered, because I felt that the friendship had to be on my terms. Now, don't get me wrong, there are some friendships that developed that were truly designed by God to help me see me. Those friendships turned into extended family for me.

The friendships that suffered from my desire to always be in control could have truly been very valuable and meaningful relationships, but they didn't. My issues were truly to blame.

The common denominator was me. I had allowed my parent spirit to create a bi-product spirit that was spiraling out of serious control. I took the need of a deeper relationship with my father and desiring a father's love to trying to make the different sexships I encountered become that love. I didn't know how to stop seeking what I thought I was missing from my father. I fed my flesh different spirits of other men and this led me into desiring forbidden fruit.

FORBIDDEN FRUIT

Not every sexship I experienced was the devil's doing. We tend to give him too much credit. The multiple sexships I experienced were all of my own choice. I could have said no, left the scene, walked away, got up out of the bed and got dressed, but I DIDN'T! I wanted to experience what I voluntarily did.

My experiences range from men to women. Not proud of any of the experiences, but let me share how being so "thirsty" for one thing can lead you down a path you may not be able to handle.

Every man that I engaged in "pre-relationship" conversations would always start off platonic. You know the usually "tell me about you" stuff. But after a while the conversation would always turn into discussing sex. Now I tell anyone I am an open book. But what most didn't know my open book had secret compartments that only the right key access could open.

One experience I was in was with a guy I met on line. I want to say to those who date off line, be careful. Not everyone is bad, but not everyone means you any good either. This guy I met was a cop. Well versed, intelligent, and down to earth. I became so engaged in our conversations that I didn't notice that he was learning my weakness without me even knowing.

After a few short months of communicating, he asked me to visit him. So of course I did, but I wouldn't go without a friend. I traveled to see him, and went to his home. He was very hospitable, charming and just as engaging in person as he was via the telephone. We began to talk, kiss and then he asked the infamous question "are you ready?" Now I really didn't want to spend my first encounter with this man in his bed, but I didn't want to seem like a little girl scared to be grown.

As we were finished our moment of sex, a woman walks in. I was a little confused, but didn't question it. She began to get undressed and got in the bed with me as he got out of the bed. She began touching me and I asked what was going on and she said, "Don't fight it. I am just getting you ready." I had no clue what she meant. She then proceeded to perform oral sex on me and all I could do was cry. I tried to fight her off, but she held me down. I kicked, and pleaded her to stop. All the while he watched and smiled.

When she felt she had accomplished what she wanted, she got up and laid beside me. He then got up and instructed me to perform oral sex on her. I told him no, I am not gay or bi-sexual. His response is one I will never forget.

He pulled a gun from off the shelf and said, "Either do it or die". At that moment, that very second my life flashed before my eyes. I didn't know what to do. I begged him just to let me go, I wouldn't tell a soul, but I didn't want to do what he was asking me to do. He informed me that when he asked me if I was ready, and I said yes, that I was being prepared to be a "bottom bitch". He stated he was a pimp and he could make my life a living hell if I didn't cooperate.

So I did, all the time crying and praying for God to help me. As I was about to comply with his wishes, the woman grabbed my hand and told me to go. She said, "This is not who you are. I was once like you, looking for love, but the love I found ain't real and you don't want to be like me." She turns towards the guy and she told him, just to let me go.

He looked at me, pointed his gun directly in my face and spoke these words, "I know who you are, where you live. I am well known in this city as a cop. If you go to the police, no one will believe you and I will make your life a living hell. Leave here and never let me see you in my city again."

I jumped up barely clothed and I ran out of the room. My friend was in the living room sleep. I woke her and said, "We have to go NOW!!!!" She looked in my eyes and she knew we had to get out of there. We drove until we found a hotel so I could get myself together. She never knew what was going on in the room until I shared with her the details. We both cried together. At that moment I knew God had spared my life for a purpose.

That moment changed my life. One would think it would have pushed me further into God, but I ran further away from him. My life spiraled more out of control. But I was queen at making it look like I was in full control.

I began having sex with any and every one. When I finally got tired of whom I had become, was when I found myself involved with a man who was a drug addict.

I was totally lost. I knew I had to get my life together, because I no longer respected who I saw in the mirror.

Every encounter I had was forbidden fruit. God never sent any of those people to me. Some, I realized later were presented for me to minister to, but I tainted them the more with my perverseness. I had to pay for those people I hurt, because I was hurting. Many nights I cried myself to sleep because the souls of those I entangled with dwelled within my spirit. My spirit man was bound with so many, that all I could do was cry at night and mask myself during the day.

When I thought I was healed after some time of not interacting with anyone I met a man from my job that I began a real relationship with, or so I thought.

We rushed through the preliminaries of the relationship so quickly that I moved this man into my home with me and my young son. In the beginning, everything was like a fairy tale. He was kind, loving, attentive, and supportive. I just didn't know he introduced his representative to me instead of the real him.

As I was so smitten with what I thought was kind, he was actually angered by the demons within. His love was actually usury so he could have a place to live, because he was homeless. His attentiveness was a decoy for his controlling nature, and his supportiveness turned out to be pure greed. Let me explain.

When I met this man I never knew he had a drug problem. He never acted as if he did. But he was a closet crack smoker. There would be times he would go to work, come home and be so antsy to get out of the house that he would pick fights to leave. He didn't have a car and I did, so I would have to bundle up my son and we take him where he wanted to go. After a few times of this I was so tired of getting off work to come home to relax to have to go back out that I started letting him take my car.

He took my car alright, right to the dope man to pawn for his next fix. He would come back late at night or a few hours before I had to be at work. He would be looking spaced out, crazed even. This cycle would happen at least twice a week, but I didn't know what was going on, I thought all relationships go through issues and at that time I was just glad to be in what I thought was a "relationship."

One particular night he was in one of those "geeked" out moods and began to argue with me for no reason. We were getting ready for bed and that is when the first hit came. He slapped me because he felt I was getting smart. Then he went to the closet and retrieved a wire hanger. He twisted it up and began hitting me with it. Claiming he knew I was cheating on him. I wasn't, but he felt I was. He was so wired, that he forced me to get into a tub of hot scalding water to "cleanse" myself. After I was told to get out, he beat me with the wire hanger while I was naked. I couldn't believe I was going through this. I tried to fight back, but the more I fought the more he would hit me. Finally, he saw the whelps on my body and begin to cry. He apologized and begged my forgiveness. I didn't know what to do. I was so tired. I was so confused. I was devastated. I laid in my bed and both of us cried ourselves to sleep. Me, from being beaten and didn't know why. Him, I can't explain.

After that night, things between us were strained. I mentioned to him several times that I felt we needed to break up. He needed to move out and leave me and my son alone. He agreed, or so I thought to go live with his sister. I made arrangements to drop him off and after which, I took my son to visit his godfather.

As I was dropping him off he looked at me and said "I will always love you, and no other man can have you." He proceeded to close the door and I drove off. I knew in my heart this was the end of us and I was free of the beatings and drama. After spending a couple hours at the godfather's home, and my son was getting tired, I drove us home. All the while speaking with my son's godfather on the phone because it was late. As I walked in my apartment, I turned the light on and put my son in his bed and pulled the door up. I was still talking with his godfather and when I laughed, my world suddenly stopped. My supposedly ex-boyfriend was in my apartment. He was hiding in my coat closet and jumped out and began punching me in my head, my face, kicking me. I screamed and dropped the phone.

The next few hours were hell. I had made it to the bathroom and looked at myself in the mirror. He was beating on the door. I had managed to get a small kitchen knife somehow and had it with me in the bathroom. I was going to take my life. I didn't want to live anymore going through what I was going through. I had alienated myself from my friends, barely visited my parents and now I had a crazed man beating the crap out of me.

Then I remembered my son was sleeping in his room. I couldn't leave him. He was all I had. I managed to leave the bathroom and make it to his room. My ex was in the bedroom with the door closed. I didn't know what to do. He had took my phone, so I couldn't call a soul to help me. But to my surprise, yet again God had spared my life. My son's godfather had called the police after hearing me scream. What seemed like hours was really minutes and there was a knock at the door.

The police had arrived and standing behind them was my son's godfather. I fell in his arms and cried. I didn't care what the police did with him, I just wanted to get my baby and get out of there.

The next day I had to go to work. My face, bruised, swollen, and distorted from being beaten. As I walked in the office, I had to face co-workers, clients, and visitors. The looks I received were that of pity. I felt ashamed and dreaded my son seeing me. I left work and vowed that I was done with love. I needed to heal and that is when I went back to God.

PREACHING WOLF

Some time had passed and I began going to a church that I felt could help me heal from everything I had put myself through and what others had done to me. I believed in God and knew he was real. I needed to find myself and I felt that giving my life back to God he would put people in my life that would guide me to who I was to become.

I had been attending this church and the pastor and wife were both sincere people. They believed in helping the community and helping every man. I was beginning to smile again. I wasn't very trusting, but I felt God had led me to this church I could trust the man and woman of God. That led me to become involved in ministry. I began working with the pastor as he was in need of an administrative assistant. I enjoyed my duties and appreciated the opportunity to serve.

One particular Sunday after service I was finishing up some paperwork in the pastors study. It was a small church, so there wasn't much office space. The majority of the congregation had left and only a few were tidying up the church. The pastor came in and closed the door. I stood up to let him have his office back and he said, no don't go. I need to speak with you.

I thought I had done something in error and was a little concerned. I sat on the opposite side of his desk and he began to tell me that I was doing a great job and how appreciative he was to have me. He then began to say something that totally blew my mind.

He looked at me, as he stood and asked me to help him unbutton his shirt. I didn't feel comfortable in what he asked me, but I trusted my leader. As I was standing in front of him he stood there and said, "Now you know as my assistant, you are not only responsible for the paperwork of the church, but also assisting me in whatever I need. Now whatever I ask you to do, I have to trust you can keep it between us. Church business is supposed to be confidential and I don't want anyone to find out that you are my favorite member." As he was speaking this, he took my hands up to the top button of his shirt and guided me to unbutton each button. He then proceeded to caress my breast and then leaned in to kiss me. I stepped backwards, grabbed my things and left without a word.

I called my friend because I needed to share what happened with someone. She instructed me to tell his wife, but I couldn't hurt her like that. I was scared and confused and really unsure of what to do.

The next week, I went back to church because I had plan on telling her. I had plan on telling the entire church and leaving never to return. But when I arrived, I was greeted by the pastor. He apologized for his actions and swore to never disrespect me again. I accepted his apology but resigned as his assistant immediately. I walked out into the sanctuary and sat down. I noticed a visitor sitting on the front row. As service proceeded, I couldn't stop looking over at the gentleman sitting on the front row. It had come time for testimony sharing and I was about to rise to testify to what had happen to me at the hands of the pastor. Before I could arise, the gentlemen stood up and asked if he could testify. He began speaking never to turn to face the audience. He said, "Pastor, I have to confess something. I did something to someone and it has haunted me for years. I beat my ex and I never got the chance to tell her I am truly sorry. I ended up in a mental institution for a short while, I was stung out on crack cocaine, and now I am healed I want to apologize to all those I have hurt in my past." Now as he was speaking the congregation was yelling, "Amen" and "Testify". He began to walk to the front of the church and turn around with his head bowed down. I sat in my seat and began to feel sick to my stomach. As he raised his head and proceeded to tell his testimony, flashes of his fist punching me came before me. It was my ex-boyfriend. I have no clue how he ended up at the same church I was but when he saw me he began to cry and called my name and asked me to forgive him. I couldn't speak, I began to shake uncontrollably, and hyperventilate severely. I had to be escorted out of the church. By the time, I made it to the doors, all I could yell was, "HE BEAT ME!"

I thought I was healed. I thought God had sent me to this church to be healed and learn how to be a better person. The opposite happened. I was fondled by the pastor and then the man who beat me was visiting the church I attended. I couldn't take it anymore. That day I left the church, I walked away from believing God loved me at all. I didn't return to that church or any church for about five years.

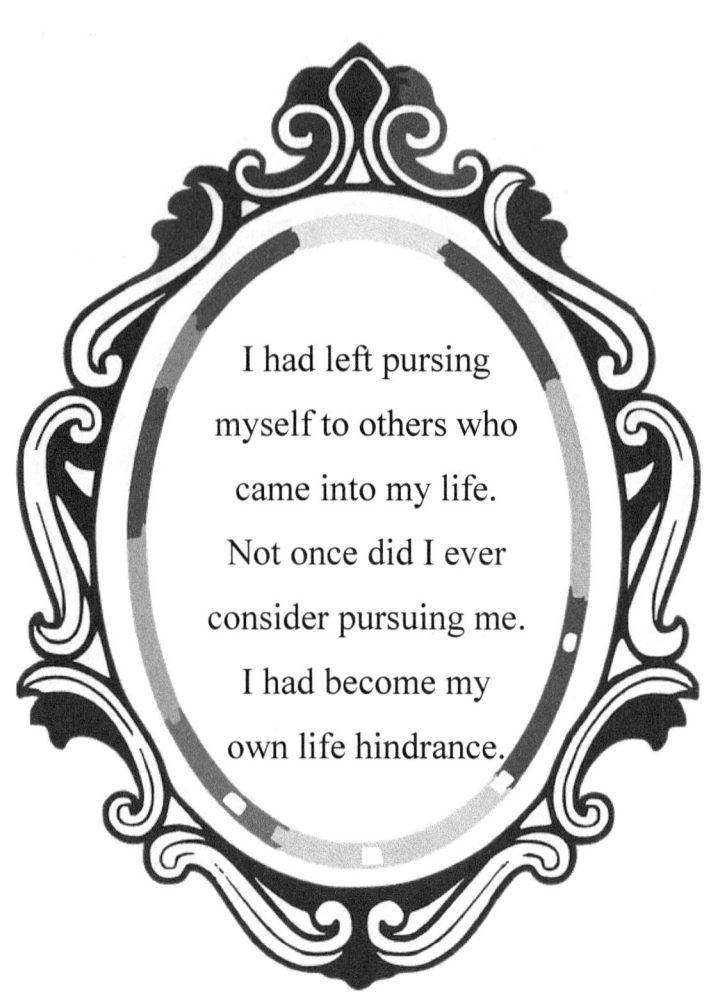

I had left pursing
myself to others who
came into my life.
Not once did I ever
consider pursuing me.
I had become my
own life hindrance.

FAUX LOVE

During this time of not attending any church, I had my second son, out of wedlock, to a man who was in wedlock… The hardest thing for anyone to hear is "I don't want you". Now He didn't say this to me, but he said it to my unborn child. I knew from that day on, I would have to take care of my boy's alone. I told myself I was prepared to do so, but I don't think I knew what that job entailed for me.

When my son turned about three years old, I met two men who we will call Tom and Harry. Tom and Harry never knew each other, but both were nice and well versed guys. The conversations I shared with each of them were different at best, however over the course of time Tom captured my heart, while Harry captured my soul. I was able to spend time with both of them individually. I grew to love them both, or what I thought was love.

Tom was a gentle man, but I could never really connect with him. We talked and shared a lot, but the connection we shared was the fact that he was in love with me and I wanted to be loved. I didn't understand that at the time he was too a broken man, not whole in some areas, but was striving to heal. We would communicate and share with each other, but at best deep down I knew that no matter how many times we tried to have a relationship, I could never fully give myself to Tom. Something wouldn't allow me to connect to him. Therefore, as time went on, we ended up going our separate ways.

Harry on the other hand, not the same. Harry captured my attention. He made me believe in love and I felt that what he was telling me was the truth. Never had a reason to doubt him, but there was still the underlying questions I never asked. As time progressed Harry became a constant part of my life. We talked sporadically, each time my heart becoming more and more imbedded in him. The more I spoke with him the more I wanted a life with him. We learned so much about each other, talked about our children, jobs, issues in life, you name it we talked about it. You see Harry lived out of state so visits were not that often. The first time we met, it felt like we had known each other for years… actually we did.

That meeting we ended up having sex. I felt my soul intertwining with his. I knew this man was the one. I knew I didn't want any other man but him. I grew to love him and he loved me. What I didn't know was this connection was slowly killing me. It was taking the life out of me. I poured more of myself into becoming the woman he wanted. I wanted him to "see" me and know I was the one to share his life with. Each time we discussed relationships and if we would ever be in one, because mind you we never committed to anything, he would always say "I don't know, but I love you." I held on to the words "I love you" for dear life, like it was my last breath. Every time feeling defeated, but knowing "he loves me" and at some point, he would know where this was going between us.

As time went on I met other men, but I never let go of Harry's love. I could fall back on it when no one was there. I could remember that one night we shared and I would fall right back into love with him all over again. Harry's love was my safety net to never being alone. I could always trust that no matter what Harry loves me and one day we would be together. I held on to this hope for ten years. I knew in the back of my mind and heart that this man was never going to commit to me. I knew that even in all the growing I had did spiritually, emotionally parts of me were still broken and holding on to a love that was not growing me but daily placing me further and further into a shell. I would have moments of strong self-esteem, and then when Harry didn't know where we stood I would go into a mini depressed state. I would pretend my world was alright, but I was no one new how bad off I really was. I didn't know how bad off I was.

Fast forward.. ten years…10 years.. of a repeated cycle. I repeated heard "I don't know, but I love you." I held on to hope that one day Harry would fully invest his life, time and love in me. I had become so depended upon hearing him say "I love you" that I never told myself. I lost who I was and the last conversation we had was like the very first real conversation we had about us, and it ended with "I don't know, but I love you." At that moment something in me clicked. I knew I had to save me. I had to gather what was left of who I was and take her away from this never ending, life draining cycle. I had walked away many times before, always to return because I thought love was real. This time, I knew love was real, I loved me. I finally realized that I loved me more than hearing the words I love you from someone who didn't understand the weight of the words. I knew I deserved more, I knew that I wanted more and that day I realized I wanted all of me back whole and healed. I had to go through this process of pursuing myself.

PURSUING ME

That was the hardest thing to do was walk away. I had invested ten years of me into someone who never took the time to nurture the investment. It was easy to hide behind words, and eloquent phrases, but reality had set in and I discovered that my investment was never going to yield me a return. I had place too many expectations in someone who never was expected to perform. I thought that my investment into him would produce what I needed within myself. I wasn't pursued by him in all aspects of life. It was easy back then to pursue me physically because I thought it would turn into pursuing me emotionally, mentally, and spiritually. It never did and I was left empty. Not by his hand, but by me emptying myself out for him to pick and choose the parts of me he wanted to use. To this day I don't blame Harry, I thank him. It made me to become responsible for me in totality.

I had left pursing myself to others who came into my life. Not once did I ever consider pursuing me. I had become my own life hindrance. I was waiting for "a man" to give me what I should have been giving myself years ago… My own self-worth, my own self-love, my own opportunity to live life at my fullest potential. I don't blame Harry, actually I thank him. It is because of him I am able to see me. I see the lack of love I neglected to give myself. I see the absence of fulfilling my purpose waiting on someone else to give me permission to, I see the emptiness I held on to, pretending I was full. I left who I was to pursue who I thought others wanted me to be. I ended up right back where I started, at the beginning.

I had to make up in my mind that I was going to purse me. I didn't know where to begin, I just had to begin. I had to discover what I didn't know about myself. This took me spending time with myself. It also took me being very honest with myself and unbelieving the lies, opinion, and perceptions others had either told me, or spoke about me. I had to begin to love myself in a real genuine way. I begin journaling my daily outcome of my thoughts towards myself, my accomplishment big or small, and my fears. I had to be honest with the person within, because getting to know me was the key to becoming who I am today.

If pursuing you is important to you, you are in a place where you have to start over again. Actually you are in a good place to do so. This time you won't allow yourself to take yourself for granted. You won't mishandle you, to be able to handle someone else. You won't allow your value to be devalued by your own self-inflicted sabotage. You will fight for you. You will learn to take time to listen to you, you thought wasn't ready to be heard. And in listening you will discover that you are enough. You are so valuable that your biggest investor will be you!

Pursuing you is a daily process. Yes you will get mad, even frustrated with you, but never give up on you again. I had to take a long hard look at me as realize that all this time I had been living for other people and never truly lived for myself. I was dying on the inside trying to make sure others stayed alive. I had to fight for myself so I could live. And guess who won this time… I did! And you can too. You have already one. Your life won't be the same after you discover you. Don't be ashamed of who you really are, but embrace her, embrace him and let you live. You will soon see that pursuing you was worth it. The second half of this book is a journal to help you begin to pursue you. Let's take this journey together… because

IT'S NEVER TOO LATE TO....

- ✓ Forgive YOURSELF
- ✓ Forgive the person who hurt you
- ✓ Start over
- ✓ Create healthy relationships
- ✓ Say I'm Sorry
- ✓ Put your past in your past

It is with the most sincere prayer that what was shared blesses you to pursue you in a real way. Discovering who you are won't be easy, and it will hurt at times but no matter what don't give up on you. Become your **BEST LOVED SELF**. Discover the power that resides within you, and watch your life flourish with endless possibilities. Your life is limitless, don't be the one who limits who you are destined to be.

With Love,
Stephanie

ABOUT THE AUTHOR

S tephanie L. Williams is certainly a visionary of great faith who consistently strives to fulfill her mission on a consistent basis. She is the CEO/ Founder of RISE Management & Consulting Firm. With over twenty years of business and leadership experience, she has combined her passion and knowledge of business, writing and consulting to help individuals to become their "best loved self."

An authentic author, Stephanie has written, co-written and edited several books to include, "Finding Eve…but where is Adam?," and, "Take me as I am" a novella. She possesses a distinct message of fortitude, faith and freedom through serving others, which has been proven to many audiences in trainings, services, consultations and within the community. She received her Bachelor of Arts degree in Legal Studies from American Public University. She is the founder of The 180 Mentoring program, helping young men turn their life in the right direction. Her philosophy of life is striving to become your best self, never to allow anyone's opinions nor perceptions to hinder you from becoming whom you were destined to be in life. She is a firm believer in this statement, "You can't love anyone until you love yourself first."

She is committed to serve as she continues her mission in helping people to pursue and live in purpose. Stephanie is a proud mother of two sons, currently resides in Dallas, Texas. Her hobbies include her love of reading, teaching, listening to music and mentoring people.

www.ingramcontent.com/pod-product-compliance
Lightning Source LLC
Chambersburg PA
CBHW061506170626
46811CB00004B/1620